Where on Earth

Is My Bagel?

By Frances Park
and Ginger Park

Illustrated by Grace Lin

LEE & LOW BOOKS Inc.
New York

Joe's
To-Go Bagels

Manufactured in China
Book design by Cathleen O'Brien
Book Production by The Kids at Our House

The text set in Xavier Medium
The illustrations are rendered in gouache

10 9 8 7 6 5 4 3
First Edition

Library of Congress Cataloging-in-Publication Data
Park, Frances.
Where on earth is my bagel? / by Frances Park and Ginger Park ;
illustrated by Grace Lin.—1st ed.
p. cm.
Summary: When a young boy in Korea dreams of eating a New York bagel,
he asks a farmer, a fisherman, a beekeeper, and a baker for help.
ISBN: 1-58430-033-7
[1. Bagels—Fiction. 2. Cookery—Fiction. 3. Korea—Fiction.] I. Park, Ginger.
II. Lin, Grace, ill. III. Title.
PZ7.P21977 Wh 2001   [E—dc21   2001023429
ISBN-13: 978-1-58430-033-5

To Justin, my sweet Godbaby —F.P.

To Ip and Ho, my big and little bagel lovers —G.P.

To Aaron who introduced me to the New York bagel,
and to Jen who showed me the New York donut —G.L.

Once there was a boy named Yum Yung who lived in a village where the mountains met the sky. There were waterfalls rushing into streams of darting fish. There were lilacs gently blossoming on every hillside.

But there were no New York bagels!

How a New York bagel popped into Yum Yung's
head was a mystery. Perhaps it came to him in a
dream, smothered with cream cheese. Or maybe
he heard sparrows singing of bagel crumbs in
Central Park.

However it happened, Yum Yung could not
stop thinking about a golden brown bagel with
a curious hole in the middle. The very idea made
his tummy growl and his mouth water.

Yum Yung declared:

"I want a bagel!"

Now dreaming about a New York bagel and actually eating a New York bagel were worlds apart.

Yum Yung wondered, "Where can I find a bagel?" He wondered and wondered, until he came up with an idea. "I will send a message!" he said.

So he sat on a rock and began to write:

Dear New York,

I would like to order one bagel to go. Please send it to me as soon as possible.

Respectfully yours,
Yum Yung in Korea

Yum Yung carried his message to a mountaintop where birds flocked. Soon a pigeon landed on his shoulder. Yum Yung tied his message to the bird's tiny leg and the pigeon flew off into the clouds.

"Pigeon," he cried out, "please return with my bagel!"

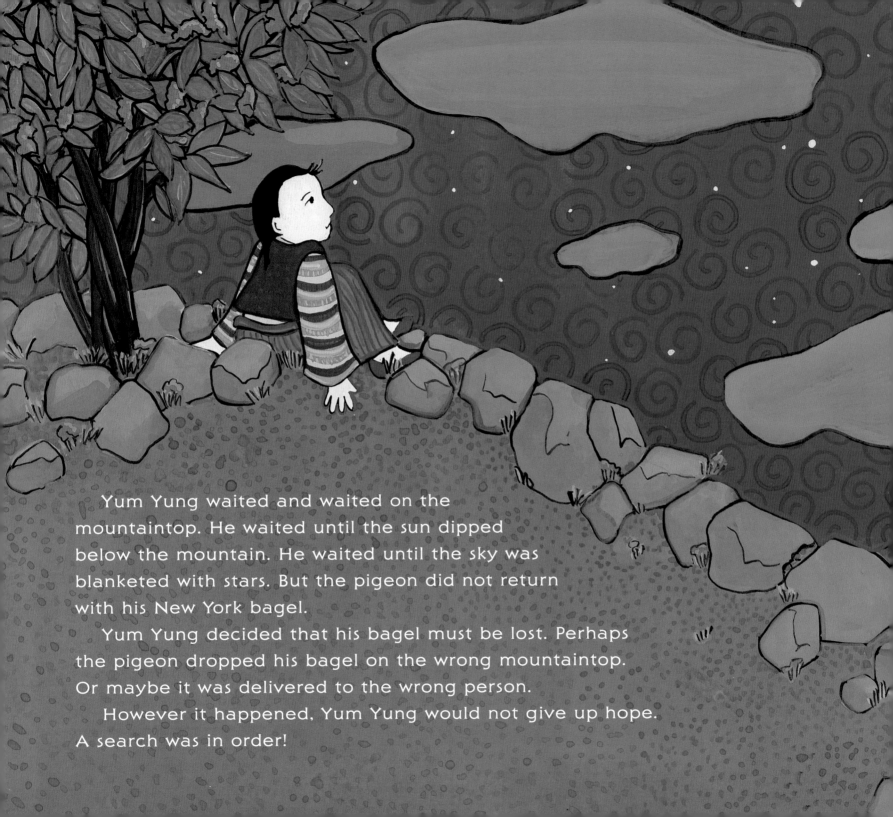

Yum Yung waited and waited on the
mountaintop. He waited until the sun dipped
below the mountain. He waited until the sky was
blanketed with stars. But the pigeon did not return
with his New York bagel.

Yum Yung decided that his bagel must be lost. Perhaps
the pigeon dropped his bagel on the wrong mountaintop.
Or maybe it was delivered to the wrong person.

However it happened, Yum Yung would not give up hope.
A search was in order!

Yum Yung declared:

"Where on Earth is my bagel?"

The next morning Yum Yung visited Farmer Ahn, who was pushing his plow in a field of wheat.

"Excuse me, Farmer Ahn," Yum Yung said. "Have you seen my missing bagel?"

Farmer Ahn wiped the sweat off his forehead. "Bagel? What in a farmer's field is a bagel?"

"It is round and it has a hole in the middle," Yum Yung explained.

"Hmm," Farmer Ahn said with a nod. He pointed to his plow wheel. "Is that a bagel?"

Yum Yung frowned. "No, that is not my bagel."

"I am sorry, Yum Yung," Farmer Ahn said. "I know about wheat that grows from the rich brown earth, but I know nothing about bagels."

Next Yum Yung visited Fisherman Kee, who was on his boat shaking slippery fish out of his net.

"Excuse me, Fisherman Kee," Yum Yung shouted. "Have you seen my missing bagel?"

Fisherman Kee threw his net back into the water with a splash. "Bagel? What in the salty sea is a bagel?"

"It is round and it has a hole in the middle," Yum Yung explained.

"Oh," Fisherman Kee said with a nod. He pointed to his life ring floating below. "Is that a bagel?"

Yum Yung frowned. "No, that is not my bagel."

"I am sorry, Yum Yung," Fisherman Kee said. "I know about fish that swim in the sea, but I know nothing about bagels."

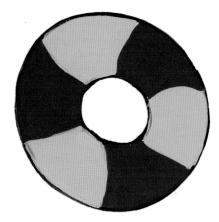

Next Yum Yung visited Beekeeper Lee, who was collecting honey from a beehive.

"Excuse me, Beekeeper Lee," Yum Yung hollered from a distance. "Have you seen my missing bagel?"

Beekeeper Lee raised her bee veil. "Bagel? What in the sweet name of honey is a bagel?"

"It is round and it has a hole in the middle," Yum Yung explained.

"Ah," Beekeeper Lee said with a nod. She pointed to the thick swarm of bees circling over her head. "Is that a bagel?"

Yum Yung frowned. "No, that is not my bagel."

"I am sorry, Yum Yung," Beekeeper Lee said. "I know about the buzzing business of bees, but I know nothing about bagels."

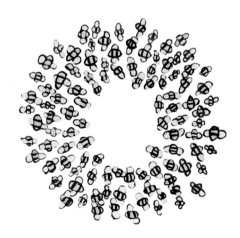

Yum Yung sat down on a quiet hillside and moaned. All hope for a bagel seemed lost!

Then a delicious smell tickled his nose. He sniffed curiously. Where was it coming from?

Yum Yung looked into the valley and blinked with delight.

There was Oh's Heavenly Bakery!

Yum Yung rushed into Oh's Heavenly Bakery, where Baker Oh was making one of her famous rice cakes.

"Baker Oh," Yum Yung pleaded, "please tell me you have my missing bagel!"

Baker Oh sprinkled a few pine nuts on the rice cake. "Bagel? What in a baker's kitchen is a bagel?"

"It is round, and it has a hole in the middle," Yum Yung explained.

"I am very sorry, Yum Yung," Baker Oh said. "I have not seen your missing bagel. But maybe that pigeon tapping at the window has better news for you."

Baker Oh opened the window. The bird flew in and landed on Yum Yung's shoulder—with a message!

While Baker Oh fed the pigeon rice cake crumbs, Yum Yung read the message aloud.

Dear Yum Yung,

Thanks a million for your order of one bagel to go. I'm real sorry, but my bagels only stay fresh on the same day they're made. So I'll do the next best thing and send you the secret recipe for my number one New York bagel!

Good luck!

Joe

From Joe's To-Go Bagels

P.S. recipe on other side

Baker Oh studied the recipe, then frowned.

"I am afraid I do not have all the special ingredients to make a New York bagel, Yum Yung. My sweet rice cakes are made with rice, sugar, and water. This bagel calls for flour, sea salt, and honey."

Yum Yung jumped. "Did you say flour, sea salt, and honey?"

"Yes," Baker Oh replied.

"I will return!" Yum Yung promised.

And indeed he did return—with Farmer Ahn and Fisherman Kee and Beekeeper Lee.

"I have the flour!" exclaimed Farmer Ahn.

"I have the sea salt!" exclaimed Fisherman Kee.

"And I have the honey!" exclaimed Beekeeper Lee.

It was time to make a New York bagel!

Baker Oh tied an apron around Yum Yung's waist. Following the recipe, Yum Yung instructed Farmer Ahn to sift flour into a mixing bowl. He instructed Fisherman Kee to sprinkle in the sea salt. He instructed Beekeeper Lee to spoon in the golden honey. Then Baker Oh poured in the water and tossed in a pinch of yeast.

Yum Yung kneaded the fragrant dough and formed it into a ring shape. He perfected the edges, especially for the hole in the middle. He dropped the dough into a large pot of simmering water. Minutes later, it floated to the top.

Then Yum Yung sprinkled it with sesame seeds, and into the oven it went.

Yum Yung watched the dough magically puff higher and higher until it nearly filled the whole oven—until it was a golden brown bagel!

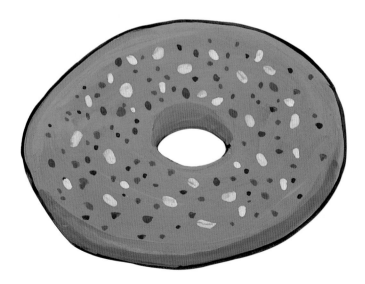

The bagel was so big that Farmer Ahn, Fisherman Kee, Beekeeper Lee, and Baker Oh had to help Yum Yung carry it out of Oh's Heavenly Bakery. They all grunted as they set the bagel down under a persimmon tree on the quiet hillside. Yum Yung broke off a piece of the bagel for each of his friends.

"Hmm!" said Farmer Ahn.

"Oh!" said Fisherman Kee.

"Ah!" said Beekeeper Lee.

"Mmm!" said Baker Oh.

The moment had finally come for Yum Yung to eat his New York bagel.

He closed his eyes and took his first bite. It was a perfect bagel with a hint of honey so sweet it made him sigh. It was soft and plump and chewy and delicious all in one bite. It was so heavenly he could even taste the curious hole in the middle!

Yum Yung declared:

"At last I have my bagel!"